This
igloo
book belongs to

....

....

igloobooks

*Published in 2014
by Igloo Books Ltd
Cottage Farm
Sywell
NN6 0BJ
www.igloobooks.com*

Text and Illustrations © Sally Hunter, 2011

www.humphreys-corner.com

*HUN001 0714
4 6 8 10 9 7 5
ISBN 978-0-85734-341-3*

Printed and manufactured in China

Humphrey's Christmas

Sally Hunter

It was Christmas Eve and Lottie and Humphrey were very excited. They had been busy helping to get ready for Christmas.

Lottie had put the icing and the snowman on the cake.

Humphrey had helped Daddy carry the
logs for the fire and Baby Jack had tried
to help wrap some presents.

Then it was time to get ready
to go to the Christmas play!
Mummy made sure they were
all wrapped up warm.

Mummy, Baby Jack, Lottie, Humphrey and Daddy set off down the hill... scrunch, crunch. Everywhere was all white and sparkly.

It was busy and noisy at the village hall.
Everyone was getting ready.
Lottie was very pleased she was the fairy.
Humphrey was a reindeer, but he said he
wanted to be the snowman next time.

Humphrey, Lottie and the other children sang a Christmas song. All the mums and dads said, "Aaah," and clapped lots.

On the way home, Daddy stopped
in the park to show Lottie and
Humphrey the stars.

Lottie said they were extra twinkly because
it was a special day. Humphrey picked the
brightest star and made a wish.

Then everyone walked home.
Humphrey and Lottie made
big steps in the snow.

Mummy made everyone a nice cup of hot chocolate.

Daddy read Lottie and Humphrey a
Christmas story about a magic snowman.

Then Humphrey and Lottie put up their stockings.

They put out a treat for Santa...

... and a carrot for the reindeer!

Lottie and Humphrey got ready for bed.

Humphrey gave
Mop an extra
big hug.

Off to sleep, little Humphrey. Goodnight.

Lottie tucked up her babies,
Trevor, Bear and Barry.

Close your eyes, Lottie. Santa only comes if you are asleep!

It was Christmas Day!
Humphrey and Lottie's stockings
were full of presents!

Humphrey and Lottie took their last presents downstairs to open with Mummy, Daddy and Baby Jack.

Humphrey was very pleased because he got the big, blue train he really wanted from the toy shop.

Lottie squealed when she saw her fairy palace!

Baby Jack liked his big, new, soft bear... and he liked the box, too!

Everyone played happily together. What a lovely Christmas Day!

Everyone played happily together. What a lovely Christmas Day!